# The Power of Empathy

## Be the Friend You've Always Wanted

By **Ruth Maille**
Art by **Remesh Ram**

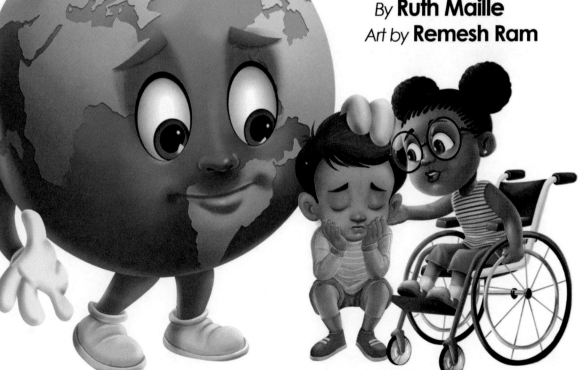

Illustrations by Remesh Ram
Designed by Praise Saflor

Publisher's Cataloging-in-Publication data

Names: Maille, Ruth, author. | Ram, Remesh, illustrator.
Title: The power of empathy : be the friend you've always wanted /
Ruth Maille; illustrated by Remesh Ram.
Description: Bristol, RI: Orbit Publishing, 2022. | Summary: Orbit visits children
at a park and teaches them about friendship and empathy.
Identifiers: LCCN: 2022918207 | ISBN: 978-1-955299-11-4 (hardcover) |
978-1-955299-10-7 (paperback) | 978-1-955299-09-1 (ebook)
Subjects: LCSH Empathy--Juvenile fiction. | Friendship--Juvenile fiction. | BISAC JUVENILE
FICTION / Social Themes / Emotions & Feelings | JUVENILE FICTION / Social Themes /
Friendship | JUVENILE FICTION / Social Themes / Self-Esteem & Self-Reliance |
JUVENILE FICTION / Social Themes / Values & Virtues
Classification: LCC PZ7.1.M346825 Po 2022 | DDC [E]--dc23

# Dedication

To every child who has ever longed
for a caring friend. You have the superpower
to be that caring friend for anyone you meet.
That superpower is called Empathy.

# A Letter from the Author

Hello friends,

Are you wondering why Orbit has two band-aids on his head?
You see, Orbit was born during the pandemic when our world was hurting. Just like when you get hurt, sometimes putting a band-aid on your boo-boo helps to make you feel better. Orbit's band-aids remind us that his adventures are about helping our world heal by teaching children ways to make life better for themselves and the people around them. He wants every child to know how they can play a big part in healing our world by spreading positivity, kindness, and love. Orbit knows he can't heal our world by himself. He needs every child to join him on his adventures so that together we can make the world a more loving and kind place in which to live.

Love

*Ruth*

Orbit arrives at the park and is greeted with shouts of excitement. "I am happy to see you!" Orbit says cheerfully.

"Orbit, we love your stories!" shouts Molly. "What are you going to talk to us about today?"

5

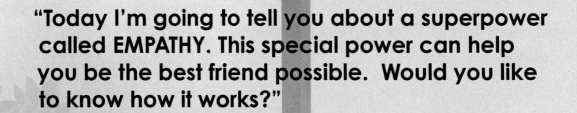

"Today I'm going to tell you about a superpower called EMPATHY. This special power can help you be the best friend possible. Would you like to know how it works?"

"YES!" the children shout.
Orbit pumps his fist

7

"Does anyone know what empathy is?" Orbit asks.
"I think I know," says Trent. "Empathy means understanding—
and also caring—how someone else is feeling."
"Excellent!" says Orbit.

8

"Empathy is also being able to see things from the other person's point of view," says Gabby. "That's right" says Orbit.

"Here's another example," says Orbit. "Have you ever felt sad if your friend was crying because they missed their mom or dad? Even though this had nothing to do with you, you still felt sad for them. That's empathy."

Gabby waves her hand in the air.
"Oh, so when my brother was sad because he didn't make the catch at his baseball game, and I felt sad for him, that was empathy?"

"Yes," says Orbit. "People feel better if they know that someone understands and cares about them."

11

"But empathy is not only about sad times;
it can be about happy times too," says Orbit.
"Can anyone think of a time when you felt happy
for someone else just because they felt happy?"

12

"I know," shouts Trent.
"Last week, my friend Kim went to the zoo. When she told us all about the animals, her excitement made me happy that she was able to go."
"Wow, great example, Trent."

13

"Can anyone think of a time when you felt angry or sad for someone else?"

Noah speaks up. "I was angry at my dog, Bandit, when he ran off with my favorite book. I yelled at him. The look on his face made me feel bad. Then he dug up my book in the backyard. I felt excited to have it back!"

14

Orbit nods and says, "Thanks, Noah. We *can* feel empathy for our animal friends too. By the way, Bandit is an excellent name for a puppy who likes to take things."

15

"You have shared great examples of empathy," says Orbit.
"I hope you can see that when we feel empathy,
we can have a lot of different emotions."
Dominic waves his hand .
"Why is it so important to talk about our emotions?"

"Good question! Talking about our emotions helps us understand why we feel the way we do. It's normal and okay to feel many different emotions."

"It's nice to feel happy emotions—like joy and excitement," says Orbit. "But it's also okay to feel unhappy emotions—like sadness, anger, and anxiety. One way to help understand your emotions is by paying attention to your body signals."

"Have you ever had a funny feeling in your stomach when you were scared?"
"Yes," answer the children.
"When you are excited, does your body feel jumpy and tingly?"
"Yes!" They all shout.

19

"Let's make a list of the different emotions that YOU remember feeling," says Orbit.
Everyone's hands wave in the air as the children shout:

"Great list! Can anyone think of a time you felt so many emotions at once that you thought you might just pop like a balloon?"

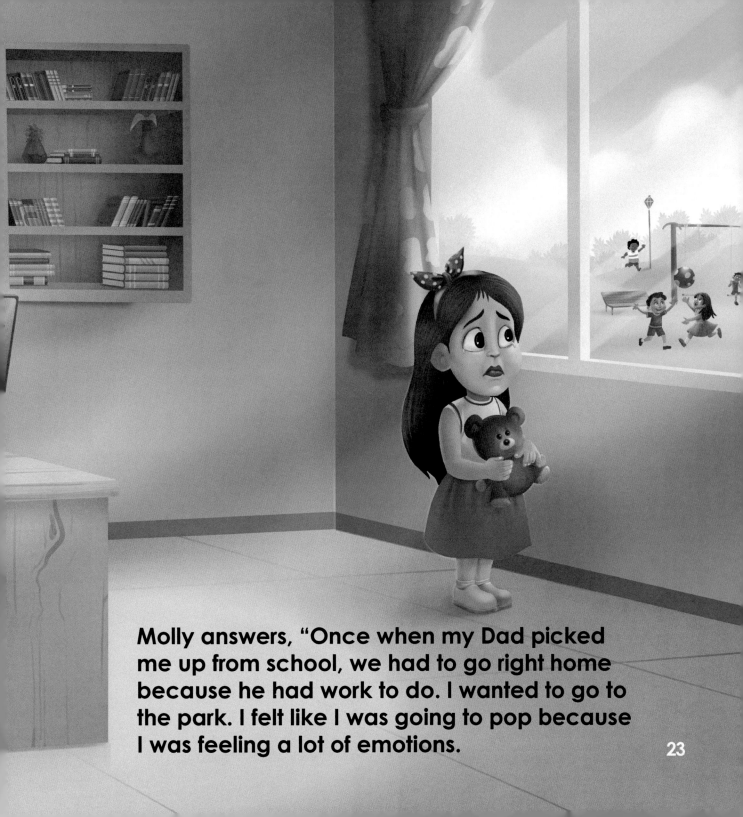

Molly answers, "Once when my Dad picked me up from school, we had to go right home because he had work to do. I wanted to go to the park. I felt like I was going to pop because I was feeling a lot of emotions.

23

Orbit understands. "When that happens to me, it helps for me to say the phrase, '*I feel___*' and fill in the blank with the emotion I am feeling."

"What are some emotions Molly could have used to fill in the blank?"
"*Disappointed?*" asks Dominic.
"*Angry,*" says Matilda.
"*Sad,*" says Trent.

25

Orbit smiles. "I'm so proud of all of you for being able to understand what Molly was feeling. That's empathy! Molly, what would have happened if you had used the 'I feel' sentence?"

I guess if I had told y Dad I felt sad he would have given e a hug. Instead, just pouted."

"Yes," says Orbit. "Maybe your Dad was also sad about not being able to spend time with you at the park."

27

"We've talked about giving empathy," says Orbit,
"but have you ever received empathy?"
"Yes!" shouts Dominic. "When I broke Kim's crayon,
I felt ashamed. She showed empathy by understanding
it was an accident. That made me feel better."

Gabby shared, "When I was excited about having ice cream with my grandpa, Trent said he was happy for me, even though he didn't go. That made me feel good."

"Empathy is a caring superpower," says Orbit.

"I think I am going to use
Empathy as MY superpower!" shouts Noah.
"Me too!" shout the other children.

"Make empathy one of your superpowers.
We all need to practice showing empathy—
to ourselves, our family, and our friends.
Until our next visit, be the friend you
want others to be to you!"

# About the Author

Ruth Maille is the author of the multi-award-winning books in *The Power of...* series. Her interactive books focus on character traits that are essential to social and emotional learning. Ruth's passion for writing comes from years of reading children's books and seeing their resulting impact on young lives. She became an author to help children learn to use their imaginations to embark on make-believe adventures that teach them lifelong values and inspire them to be anything they choose.

Ruth has owned and operated a daycare/preschool for 32 years and is a certified parent-relationship coach. She is grateful each day for the privilege of working with so many families.

# About the Illustrator

Remesh Ram is the co-founder of Prayan Animation Studio, with over 15 years of experience in the animation & illustration industry. He led Prayan Animation Studio for a glorious ten years. Along with his team of illustrators, they work together to bring stories to life with their beautiful and eye-catching illustrations

# For more award-winning books by Ruth Maille, check out the books below.

If you enjoyed *The Power of Empathy Be the Friend You've Always Wanted*, we would love to hear from you. Reviews are incredibly valuable to authors. Please consider leaving a review on Amazon or Goodreads.

**Share a picture on social media**
@Orbitkindnesschallenge.

Made in the USA
Middletown, DE
09 May 2023

30317291R00022